Table of Contents

Spanish Glossary

Gracias dìos – Thank you God 4

No sè tarde – Don't be late 5

No lo hàre – I won't 5

Tudos lo què los hombres quìeren estu culo gordo- All men want is your fat ass 5

Voy a decir què estoy cansado- I'm going to say I'm tired 5

Hola. Que estas hacienda- Hi, what are you doing? 6

No puedo hablar en este momento- I can't talk right now 6

¿Por què? – Why, Because 6

Què – What, who, that 6

Mi maquillaje – My makeup, put on makeup 6

Perfecto – Perfect 9

¿Ahora puedo hacerte una pregunta? Can I ask you a question? 10

Pequeña la concha – Little Shell 11

Sì – Yes 11

Gracìas por todo lo què has hecho por mì – Thank you for what you've done for me 23,24

De nada yo buscado hacerte tu sentir Bueno – My pleasure, I wanted to make you feel good 23,24

Lo hiciste bien, papa muy bien – You did goo (pap slang for daddy), very good 23.24

Yo realmente me gustas. Tienes que creer me, no pasa nada entre nosotros- I really like you, believe me there's nothing going on between us 26,27

Irse- To leave 26,27

Mira, no vuelvas llamarme! – Look, Don't tell me again 31,32

Hola – Hello 31,32

Las Hermana – sisters 33.34

Tia- Aunt 33,34

Niños- child, children 33,34

Ti ti – Auntie 33,34

Universidad – University 33,34

Pablo de Olividad – (Part of the University) 33,34

Hola – Hello 34,35

¿Nada mam y tu? – Nothing mommy you?34,35

Pero bien – but fine 34,35

Yo – I, me 35,36

Muy Bien – Very good 35,36

Què su padre – that, his father 35.36

4

Hermanas pasando tiempo con sus padre – Sisters spending time with their father 35.36

Padre – father 35.36

Va basta! – Enough 36.37

¿Què esta teniendo relaciones sexuales con? – Who are you having sex with? 36,37

Conchilla – Shell 38,39

Hola ti ti, hola madre – Hello aunti, hello mother 41.42

Madre – Mother 41,42

Jovencito – youngster 41,42

Hola – Hello 41,42

Tìa – Aunt 42,43

Padre, Madre, - Father, Mother 43,44

Miguel, conozco tu frusterated con migo, la calma pero bajaràstu- I know your upset with me, but you'll calm down 43,44

Tono cuando mè hables – tone when you speak to me 43.44

Lo siento madre, la mamà- Sorry mother, mom 43.44

Madre, la mama- Mother, mom 45.46

Miguel – Michael 46,47

Madre, la mama – Mother, mom 46,47

La amìga – Friend (female) 46.47

A tu casa de madres – to your mother's house 46,47

Madre, la mama – Mother, mom 46.47

The Unexpected

By: R.J. Voice

September 30, 2017

The Vision

The room was dark as night, she and one other person was in this room. She was on her knees with her head down to the floor as if she were an ostrich eating from the ground. She was the only one wearing a pink and white flower in her hair. While her head was down, she turned and saw the bottom of a door sill open. She focused on his feet as he walked through the door. He wore black dress shoes and black dress pants. She never saw his face only the hem of his pants. He reached toward her face with both hands and gently pulled her head to his mouth and

whispered in her ear. "You will always hear my voice." He

gently released her head then she put her face in her hands

to hide the despair it would show, but a black butterfly

appeared about three feet away as he walked out of the

door and a light shined in the room from the window of that

door. She was able to see, not only the door sill, but a

window that was a part of the door once she lifted her head.

She favored him with a bright smile. The light was the only

thing shining in the room other than her pink and white

flower and later her smile

CHAPTER ONE

A Look of Interest

Since she loved music, teaching and butterflies, she noticed

one in the top left corner of the door. A black butterfly, the

only one in his office. Mayonna Conchilla walked out of

Dr. Michael Benjamin Taylor's office. Down the hall she

heard him say, *"Gracias, dios, she said yes."*,she noticing

his excitement to her response of him asking her to dinner.

She smiled and continued to walk down the hallway to her

classroom to continue to pack her things. Great things

were beginning to happen for Mayonna. She was hired by

a company in the U.S. to travel to Costa Rica, all expenses

paid, including her housing to teach the Spanish youth to

play jazz music for couple of years. She hated to turn in

her two weeks' notice to Dr. Taylor because she enjoyed

her job but knew she could not pass up the opportunity and

felt at peace after she did. Mayonna finished putting away

the instruments used by her last class of the day. Violins in

the right corner, trumpets in the left corner and keyboards

hanging at the very top of the wall in the center of the classroom.

Dr. Taylor walked in the room while she was packing and said to her, "Mayonna, you said yes to my invitation for dinner, but you didn't give me your phone number?"

"I'm sorry, it feels a little awkward going on a date with my boss. I ended an abusive relationship, and finalized the divorce, it may be too soon for me."

"You're not my employee anymore, remember? You turned in your two weeks' notice and take your time I don't want to rush you into anything." She grabbed his hand and guided him to her desk in her classroom, picked up a black ink pen and wrote her phone number in the palm of his hand. 502- 555-7777. She never spoke a word, but she slowly closed his hand after writing her number. She looked him in his eyes and said;

"Call me tonight around eight o'clock."

"I had hoped I could pick you up tonight around 7 o'clock, if you don't mind."

She looked at him and responded;

"You're pretty straight forward, but I don't mind." She picked up her red and tan purse from her desk chair and walked out of the classroom toward the lobby of the office. She opened the lobby door, while holding the handle with her right hand. Looking over her shoulder at Dr. Taylor and said; *"No se tarde."*

With an intense look of interest, he said; *"No lo harè."* She continued out of the lobby and down the hallway with a slight smile on her face. Down the steps to the garage and into her brand-new top of the line red Jeep Renegade. As she drives, she begins to think of million reasons to cancel the date. She began to think to herself;

"What have I done? I'm not ready to date again." *"Todos lo que los hombres quieren es tu culo gordo."* "What can he offer me"?

"When a man asks a woman out to dinner, he expects ass at the end of the night." Voy a decir que estoy cansado." She pulled in her driveway, shut off her truck. "Okay…snap out of it, I'm going in the house to take a shower, get dressed for this date, and have a good time. Who knows, he may be a very nice man." Mayonna got out of her truck, looked at her watch and saw it was already late.

CHAPTER TWO
Preparation

She only had a half hour to get ready. She rushed in the house, threw off her shoes and clothes, jumped into the shower, and shampooed her hair. She got out of the shower, brushed her teeth, walked in her bedroom, which

11

was connected to her bathroom. A towel wrapped around her she stood in front of her closet looking for something to wear. Her phone rings, she grabs it *"Hola."*

"Hola. ¿Què estas hacienda?"

"Tianna, *No puedo hablar en este momento."*

"Por que"

"Porque me voy a una cita."

"¿què?"

Mayonna loved her friend dearly, but she quickly hung up the phone, blow dried her long black hair and curled it. "Hmmm," with her index finger pressed against her bottom lip, "Since it is a warm summer evening I'll wear my white silk dress, it's comfortable, or my fitted white strapless bell bottom jump suit with my tan three strap 4 inch heel sandals." She paused for a minute, then decided; "The jumpsuit it is." She pulled it out of the closet, put it on along with her shoes when she noticed something. She shouted aloud "*Mi maquillaje.*" She rushed in her bathroom and applied her makeup neatly. She looked in the mirror and said; "Perfecto!" She sprayed a nice perfume mist, with a fresh scent of powder. As she squirted the last bit of perfume, she looked at the clock and it saw it was time. Her doorbell rang. She quickly clutched her white and goldish tan purse, stood by the front door, fluffed her hair, took a deep breath, and opened…

There he was standing 6'4", smooth dark skin, wearing a white shirt, white pants, black belt, black dress shoes, neat haircut and smelling good. She thought to herself; clean dressed. *We're matching, and he has nice shoes, I love a man who smells good with nice shoes.*

"Hello Mayonna, you look nice."

"Thank you, you do too. "she responded."

"Are you ready to go?"

"Yes." she smiled. He extended his right arm to her. "*A gentleman?*" she thought. They walked to his latest edition of the black Mercedes truck, he opened the door for her and waits for her get in. Closed the door, got in on his side and drove off. Dr. Taylor looked at Mayonna and said, "Pick where you would like to go, anywhere, and I'll take care of it."

"Anywhere?" she responded,

"Anywhere."

"I would like to go on a large boat and have a private dinner." She said sarcastically.

"I'm calling now for private reservations."

Mayonna has a surprised look in her eyes, she never expected him to take her on a yacht for dinner. She didn't believe it.

CHAPTER THREE

The Date

They arrived on a yacht, and her phone rang, she looked at it and it was Tianna. Mayonna turned her phone off and remained calm as usual. It was a large boat, reserved for a dinner for two. Dr. Taylor got out of his truck and opened the door, Mayonna got out.

"Thank you," she said.

"Your welcome," he said.

"I was kidding about the boat ride," she said.

"You didn't think I would do it? or could do it? What were you thinking, Ms. Conchilla? " he said.

"Honestly, I didn't think you would."

"Why?" he asked, with an inquisitive look on his face. She shrugged her shoulders.

"Because, when I have been asked in the past what I want, I've never been taken serious when I answer."

"Well… I'm taking you serious," he said. They sat down at a table for two. There was a beautiful view of the water, the warm summer breeze blowing off the water was soothing. While waiting to be served, Dr, Taylor asked;

"Why is your last name little shell?' "I used to be fascinated with shells when I was a kid, so my parents changed my last name from theirs, which was Martinez to Conchilla, which means shell. They sometimes called me pequeña la concha. The waiter arrived.

"Good evening sir and maam, how may I serve you?" They both ordered a glass of wine.

 "Can I ask you a question?" she said.

"You can ask me anything you want?",

"Anything?" she said.

"Anything." he said.

"Are you Spanish?"

"No."

"Are you Spanish?" he retorted with the sound of sarcasm.

"Yes" she said, ignoring his sarcasm.

"Where did you learn to speak Spanish?" she asked him.

"I was raised in Santa Domingo, the Dominican Republic. I still have friends there; I go back and visit sometimes. You told me you were newly divorced and were abused". He said.

"I am divorced. My ex-husband was a womanizer and he physically and mentally abused me. He tried to take my children from me in the court battle, but he lost. I guess I was like any other woman who wanted to have a family, never noticed any signs, just wanted what I wanted. Unfortunately, my kids had to endure the divorce, but they

17

seem okay now. Now I'm here with great opportunities to live again, and to bring my kids into a better life." Taylor listed to her.

"We all sometimes make bad choices in life Mayonna, no one's perfect." He said.

"How did you grow up in the Dominican Republic?" she responds inquisitively.

"My mother was a black woman and my father divorced, he was a black man, she remarried when my brothers and I were little here in the U.S., she married a Dominican man, who is my stepfather. We ended up moving to his hometown and we learned Spanish while living there. When I became an adult, I decided to move back to the U.S. I'm a Black man. Why do you ask?"

"You speak Spanish pretty good and I was curious" she said.

"*¿Ahora puedo hacerte una pregunta?*" he said to her.

She smiled. "*Sì, supongo.*"

He laughed. "I can't ask you anything?" he said.

"Yes," she said kindly.

"I understand you have kids."

"I do" she said.

"Girls?.Boys? he said.

"Three girls" she held up three of her fingers.

"Do you mind if I ask you if you are still in love with their father?"

"No, not anymore. I was wondering, I have been working at the office for a year. Why are you showing interest in me now?" she said.

"Honestly, I became interested when we did our interview for the music settlement on WCRE radio. I noticed you were very genuine, and I was attracted."

Their wine arrived. Dr. Taylor and Mayonna looked at each other. He took a sip.

"How do you know if your no longer in love?" he asked.

"Because, I don't have the same feelings I use to have."

"You still see him?" he asked.

"Yes, he has visitation rights for the kids," she said. The waiter returned and asked,

"*¿Està listo para pedir señor?*"

"*Si,* Mayonna order whatever you like." They ordered their food.

"Mayonna, I'm glad you're moving forward in your career, now that I'm getting to know you more, I kind of wish you weren't going away so far" Dr. Taylor said.

"Things have been going pretty well for me, I received a great job offer and me and my kids will be moving to Costa

Rica next year. How long have you been living here in California?" she said.

"I moved here a year before I hired you." he said.

"Do you have kids, Michael?"

"Yes, I have two teenage daughters," he said.

"Yeah? I have two as well, pre-teens." She was beginning to feel a little more comfortable talking to him. Their food arrived, and they began to eat.

"It's been hard raising them alone but we're making it. She wiped the corner of her mouth with a napkin.

"How about you? How long has it been since you been in a relationship? Do you still love the woman in your most recent relationship, or your daughters mother? Why did it end?"

"You aren't shying away from the questions." Taylor laughed.

"You said ask you anything," she responded. He smiled.

"It has been nine years; I am not in love with her anymore. I wanted to marry her, but she didn't want to marry me. We both decided to end the relationship because she wanted the relationship to stay as it was, to live together as if we were married, but I didn't, so we decided to end it plus, we lost interest in one another."

"Are your kids her kids?" she said.

"No." he said.

"So, how is your relationship with your daughters' mother?" she asked.

"We communicate well regarding the girls only; I spend a lot of time with my daughters and take them to school every morning." He looked at her eating her food. She was eating fast.

"How is your food?" he said.

"It's really good. Your shrimp looks delicious.", said Mayonna.

Laughing, "You're eating it like it's good." He said. "You have sauce on your chin." He reached over the table and wiped the sauce off her chin with a napkin. "and yes, my shrimp is good. You're looking at it like you want to eat it." Laughing.

"I don't want your food; I have my own" Mayonna laughed.

"One more question, I have seen Renee watch your every move in the lobby of the music center, does she like you?" Dr. Taylor became slightly irritated that Renee's name entered their conversation.

"Renee is my last girlfriend's sister," he said.

"Yeah, she made sure that I knew you dated her sister. She literally watches your every move as if you are her man. Are you her man?" Mayonna asked.

"No, I'm not her man. She's still a friend even though her sister and I are no longer in a relationship." he said.

Mayonna wiped her mouth with a long thick white napkin.

"Are you ready to go?" Taylor asked her.

"I am" she responded. Dr. Taylor left the payment of the dinner on the table including a very generous tip. They took their time and walked to his truck. Mayonna looked at the sky and saw a beautiful full moon. "It's a lovely night out" she said.

Dr. Taylor looked at the sky then looked at her eyes.

"I agree, it is a lovely night." They made it to the truck he again opened the door for her to get in. He got in and they drove off, then they arrived at Mayonna's home, he got out and opened the door. He walked her to her door. Mayonna looked at him with a warm smile and said,

"Thank you, Michael, for the dinner it was very nice. I enjoyed the conversation and thank you for being honest with me. (Pause) You were being honest with me, right?" Mayonna looked at Michael with a smile and waited for him to respond.

" Yes, I was being honest. I have no reason not to be Mayonna. Can I call you tomorrow? I would like to talk with you and possibly take you out again," he said.

"Yes, I would like that." She responded. Michael grabbed both of her hands, kissed them softly. "Good night" she said. He stood there and waited until she completely closed the door before he walked back to his truck. Once she closed the door on the other side she leaned her head back against the door and took a deep breath. She smiled and thought to herself; *The date wasn't so bad. He's a gentleman.* She looked at her watch. It's 9:45pm. She kicked off her shoes at the front door, walked up the stairs into the bathroom, and prepared to shower.

CHAPTER FOUR
Tianna phone conversation

After Mayonna got out of the shower she moisturized herself with lavender oi, put on a t-shirt and her *pantuflas*. She checked her *la bolsa*, grabbed her phone looked at it and saw it was 4-5 missed calls from her best friend from childhood Tianna. Mayonna sent a text to her daughters to see if everything was okay with them as they were with their father for the night. The kids replied with phone texts letting her know they were fine. She was comforted in knowing all was well. She returned Tianna's call. The phone rang and Tianna picked up;

"Holaaa." The background sounded like she was at a club.

"Hola Tianna, I'm returning your call."

"*¿Quièn es el nuevo hombre del que no sè nada?*"

"*Èl es mi antiguo jefe*"

"*Estas hacienda tu jefe?*"

"*No, no estoy haciendo mi jefe y el era mi antiguo jefe?*"

"Tianna, I'm tired.

"*¿Po què?*"

"porque." Mayonna said.

"Hey... what up with this guy?" Tianna asked. Mayonna stretched back on her bed and began to think of when he asked her out and how nice was.

"Tianna, he is really a nice guy, he took me to dinner on a yacht. He asked me where I wanted to go, so, I said I want to have dinner on a boat, kidding around and he literally made reservations on the way. We had a good conversation about who he was, if he had kids, which he does, if he is still in a relationship, you know, stuff. he wants to call me tomorrow, I said yes."

"A yacht? mama he loaded like that?" Tianna asked.

"I guess."

"Mayonna you sound so nonchalant about it. You never care if a guy has money."

"Not like you Tianna", she said sarcastically.

"Does he have any friends, or a brother with money? They usually don't" Tianna continued.

"Tianna…" Mayonna said.

"No, really though, good for you mama, I want you to be happy, your young go for it, but be careful" Tianna said.

"Gracias, Tianna. I'm tired I came in from work then I immediately got ready for the date. I will talk to you later. It is so loud, where are you?"

"You know I'm at Club Conga trying to find mi nuevo hombre."

"Good night Tianna, Mayonna when do you leave for Costa Rica?"

"It's not until next year."

"So, what are you going to do for a year?" Tianna asked.

"Relax, I still get a nice salary that is a part of my contract when I was hired at the music settlement even if the contract is over. I gave a notice, which I didn't have to with the contract ending, but I did. I will have that salary to live off until I leave," Mayonna said.

"Oh, Adios mama!" Tianna replied.

"Adios Tianna!" Mayonna turned her light off pulled the cover over her head and closed her eyes. Her phone rang. (She blew out a deep loud breath) She thought it was Tianna again, she grabbed her phone and looked at it, it's Michael Taylor. She was curious to why he was calling her, plus she didn't mind talking to him again. She answered it.

CHAPTER FIVE

Michael Phone Conversation

"Hola?" she answered.

"Hola Mayonna, es Miguel"

"I thought you were going to call me tomorrow? is everything okay?" she asked him.

"Yes, it is, I thought about you on the drive home and how I really enjoyed your company and how beautiful you looked."

"Thank you, you looked good too.

Umm…Mayonna responded calmly. "It's pretty late Michael and I'm kind of sleepy" Michael interjected…

" Mayonna, do you mind if I come back over and spend more time with you? I enjoyed our evening and would like for the night to go continue."

She paused to think, then answered." Sure, why not." "We can watch a movie."

"I'll be there shortly," he said with subtle enthusiasm.

CHAPTER SIX

The Night Continued

Mayonna got up to put on a white tank top and a pair of light grey cotton shorts. She walked in the kitchen to take get cookie dough to bake some chocolate chip cookies. She pulled out her cookie sheet her friend Tianna bought her for a gift. "I never used this sheet, well... now I have a reason to use it. It seems easy enough." She sprayed the pan with cooking spray, then he placed the dough on the sheet. She turned on the oven to preheat. *"No puedo creer estoy permitiendo que estè hombre venga a mi casa esta hora de la noche. ¡Què me pasa!"* The doorbell rang ....

Mayonna went to the door and opened it... there again standing tall, dark, and handsome was Michael Benjamin Taylor. This time dressed in a white t-shirt, black sweatpants and black tennis shoes, and a black baseball hat. Mayonna stood in the door, with her hair pinned up in a banana clip. She let him in. *"Bienvenido"* She said.

Michael walked in and responded *"Gracias mi señora.*

"Are those cookies I smell?" Michael said.

"Yes, I thought we could have a snack while we watched a movie."

Michael took off his shoes at the front door. Mayonna noticed he does so while closing the door behind him. He allowed her to lead the way up the four steps, straight into her living room.

"I'm going to get the cookies I believe they are done. Help yourself to finding a movie. The remote control is on the entertainment center."

Michael sat down on her couch. He was impressed with how clean her home was and how most of her things were in place. This showed him how she lived at home, which is one of the things he was curious about. He thought it was lovely. He reached for the remote on her entertainment center and noticed she had a statue of a monarch butterfly on the top shelf, above her T.V. the butterfly was followed by a host of small butterflies of different colors on different shelves of the entertainment center.

The entertainment center was sectioned with five shelves, all with pictures of her kids, her and her friend, on her walls were her high school diploma, three of her college degrees, and her musical achievements. Mayonna walked over to the couch with a plate of cookies and two glasses, for a choice of drink.

"What would you like to drink?"

"Water is fine, thank you," he responded. She returned to the kitchen to get two bottled waters, when she returned, she asked him "So…how did you become the Director of the music settlement?" She sat down putting the water bottles on her glass cocktail table.

Michael explained. "Well… I have a bachelor's, two masters' and my PhD; all in music. I own the music settlement here in Los Angele, California and other locations including; New York, Atlanta, and one over sees in the Spain. The Director before me of this location was someone I looked up to, he taught me a lot of things about ownership. He ended up getting sick and recommended me to be the interim Director until he got well enough to go to work, but he never got well. He passed away. I stayed in the position and I was offered for it to be more permanent, thus I became the new Director of the music settlement. I was an assistant professor, teaching music classes before this position. I'm a blessed man, I've been very fortunate.

I love music, I love the sound of music, kind of like when I first heard your voice in your initial telephone interview."

"Yeah, I remember that interview" Mayonna said, "I was nervous, but you made the interview easy, like you make talking to you now, easy." They look at each other with intense attraction. Mayonna reached for the remote to look for a movie and Michael grabbed her hand.

CHAPTER SEVEN
Butterflies Emerge

Mayonna looked at Michael and he looked back at her, they slowly pulled into each other, close enough to feel each other's breath. Mayonna pulled back and turned her head in ambiguity to if she should be doing this. Michael took her chin and gently guided it toward his full lips, they kissed slowly. They explored tongues kissing in slow motion with the sound of sporadic smacking and light breathing. Michael pulled Mayonna body close to his, and wrapped his arms around her waist, while she touched the back of his head. They slowly pulled back and looked at each other. Mayonna got up from the couch, Michael was still seated. She turned around and invited him to her bedroom. He got up and followed her as if he was under a spell.

Before they could get to the bed they started kissing. He removed his t-shirt, then her tank top, and kissed her down her neck then onto her breast. He slowly licked her brown nipples in a circular motion. Her nipples popped up from the stimulation. He moved across to her right breast and licked that nipple while he softly touched her left one. He unhurried and relaxed as he worked his way down to her belly button with soft kisses. He gradually turned her over and tenderly removed the banana clip from her hair. He caressed her back and basted her ass with his tongue.

He kissed the back of her thighs then spread her legs and massaged between them. He lifted her by her waist, and guided her toward him, while he swiftly put on a condom. He sat backward. Mayonna gently slid down on his joystick. She rocked her pelvis back and forth while he held her breast from behind and kissed the side of her neck. She

37

bounced up, and down on him in a consistent motion. He moaned, "Mmmm…" and gasped for breath. His moaning sounded like melody in her ears, music sweet and complete. Their bodies were in harmony with one another every movement orchestrated, like a symphony.

He slowly removed her from himself and turned her over on her back and spread her legs. She felt his warm breath near her lips. His hands gently opened her up, and she moaned in intense pleasure. His breath got closer and the warmth of his tongue slid in, out, and around her with intermittent kisses.

"Ohhh…se siente tan bien!" she softly said. She was pleasured beyond measure. He kissed his way toward her breast and reached her aroused nipples. He spread her golden legs from each end of her room, held her ankles firmly glided his love into her pool of moisture. He consistently stroked her tenderly while they kissed each

other. They both reached an intense climax.

CHAPTER EIGHT

Stalking

He held her, while her head was placed on his chest. He

kissed her on her nose, her face, her forehead, and her lips

consistently until she woke up. She looked at him with one

eye opened, the she instantly noticed his heartbeat matched

hers. Their hearts were beating at the same pace, at the same time.

"Buenos dias." he said to her.

"Wow…still beautiful when you're waking up in the morning, even with one eye closed. Mira, it's morning" he said to her.

"You have humor in the morning?" she said to him. She paused for a minute and said, "Miguel, gracias por todo lo que has hecho por mì."

"De nada, mi placer, hacerte sentir bien."

She smiled and said "lo hiciste bien papa, muy bien." Michaels' phone rang, he looked at it and hung up. It immediately rang again, he looked at it and again hung up.

Mayonna asked him, "Are you okay?"

"Yeah, I am." he said. Seeming irritated.

She got up to go to the bathroom and his phone rang again. This time he answered it, and Mayonna overheard his conversation. "Hello, I am unavailable right now. What!! "He rushed to Mayonna's bedroom window butt naked, he saw Renee standing across the street from Mayonna's house.

"What the hell are you doing following me!" He said on the phone. Mayonna walked back in her bedroom, looked at Michael, but she was distracted by his well-endowed penis. She quickly gathered her initial thought and asked…

"What's going on Michael?" He rapidly put on his pants and his shirt. Mayonna walked toward her window. She saw Renee standing outside across from her house. Mayonna began to raise her voice and point to the window.

"Why is Renee outside my house Michael?

"I don't know." he calmly replied.

"Then why is she outside my house and where are you going?"

Michael looked Mayonna in her eyes..."I told you I dated her sister, I was friends with her family for a long time afterward. One evening Renee and I went to get something to eat, and she asked me if I believed in having friends with benefits. I told her no. She then proceeded to tell me how horny she was and asked me to sleep with her." Mayonna frowned and crossed her arms with a look of unbelief on her face.

Michael continued, "I told her she is like a sister to me, she responded to me with 'I'm not your sister, and you no longer date my sister. Mayonna, I didn't know what I was thinking at the time, but we went back to my place and had sex. That is the only time I slept with her, she has been watching me and every woman I have a conversation with ever since. She doesn't want me to have a relationship outside of her, she didn't like me dating her sister and was

42

happy when our relationship ended. I haven't had a long-term relationship since her sister!"

"I knew she liked you and I asked you. You didn't tell me you slept with her! Mayonna yells.

"I answered your questions honestly, and you didn't ask me if I slept with her, you asked if she liked me" Michael said trying to calm her down at this point.

"And… you never answered that Michael" Mayonna retorted. "I didn't want to say anything out of fear that you would respond as you are now". Michael said.

Renee screamed from across the street loud enough for Michael, Mayonna and her neighbors to hear. "and what does that mean?"

Renee yelling from outside. "Michael, you need to come out of there. All she wants from you is your money, you need to come out before I come in and get you!" Renee said. "I know she don't think she is coming in my house!

this bitch crazy! Mayonna said. Mayonna was shocked, this was something she never expected.

"What type of web are you weaving Michael!" Mayonna yells.

"Mayonna I'm not the spider. I'm the black butterfly who has gotten trapped in a web and it seems as if there's no way out!" he replied with great frustration.

"You shouldn't of fucked her, Oh, there's a way out, it's out my bedroom, down the stairs, and out my front door! Get out Michael!"

"Mayonna please…" He pleaded with her. "Don't be angry with me. I have been honest with you from the beginning!"

"Not totally Michael. You didn't tell me all of this in the beginning. I knew something was crazy about her when she stared at me at work every time you were kind towards me!" she said.

"She knew I was interested in dating you and she didn't want me to," "I may have caused her to believe the relationship was more than what it was." Michael said.

"Michael, you are a grown ass man. You can't allow a woman to control who you want to date! You need to leave!"

"Mayonna..." he said.

"Now!"

"Mayonna, you don't understand!" Michael grabbed his hat walked to the front door. His final words were while putting on his shoes, "Every time I'm interested in another woman, she finds a way to sabotage it Mayonna. *Yo realmente, realmente me gustas. Tienes que creer me, no pasa nada entre nosotros*!

"*Irse*! she firmly said with the door wide open. Michael walked out and Mayonna slammed the door.

"Damn, I knew it was too good to be true, it's always some type of drama! Why can't I meet a man who doesn't have evil and controlling women associated with him! …just when I open up to someone" Mayonna put her hands over her face, with her back against the door. She slid down to the floor, took a deep breath, and stared forward for a minute.

CHAPTER NINE
Michael Reaches Out

Saturday continued as a usual weekend day for Mayonna. She cleaned her house, went to the store, and washed her clothes. She sat at her dining room table to look at her new hire acceptance packet for her job. "A year from now I will be gone, starting my new career, in a new country" she thought to herself. She noticed she hadn't sent a piece of paperwork in the mail that should have been mailed, so she left to go to the post office. She returned home, and she heard her phone ring. She saw it was Michael. She didn't answer. She left to continue her errands for the day.

She returned home and as she walked in her house the phone rang. It was Tianna. Mayonna didn't answer. She felt sad and disappointed for allowing herself to be open to someone so fast. She felt it was too soon considering her just walking away from a bad marriage. She allowed her emotions to take over and ended in another type of messy relationship. She was afraid this would happen. She wasn't in the mood to talk to Tianna about what happened, and she wanted to put it all behind her and move on immediately. She really thought the relationship between her, and

Michael would be a good one. Her phone rang again, it was Michael.

"Should I answer it?" she thought to herself.

She thought about how he made love to her, and how good and genuine it felt. "He touched me like I was special to him," she thought. By the time she decided to answer the phone it had stopped ringing. Saturday night approached and Mayonna was tired. She had experienced a lot in the past few days. She showered then curled up in her bed to watch a movie. She fixed the channel then fell asleep. Sunday morning, Mayonna woke up, washed her face, and brushed her teeth. She ate a piece of toast and a small glass of orange juice, then she got back in the bed.

She thought about Michael most of the day, but her stubborn nature prevented her from calling him. She had only known him for a short while, but it was like she had known him for a very long time. She felt as if a part of her was missing, and she never felt this way before. She missed him. His presence, his voice, the smell of his cologne, and his strong hands. Her mind wandered if she never talked to him again if they would have ever worked in a relationship, or if she does talk to him will she have to deal with a crazy as Renee. She admitted to herself, "If he made love to her like he did me, and I had no self-control I would probably be hypnotized by the dick too. She fell asleep.

CHAPTER TEN
Monday Morning

Mayonna woke up well rested, but still had Michael on her mind. She snatched her phone and pressed the missed calls button to return the calls he made to her the previous day. His phone line rang three times; he never picked up. She hung up and tried again, it rang…rang…and rang…he finally answered.

"Hello."

"Hi Michael, it's Mayonna I'm returning your calls from yesterday."

"I thought I would never see you or talk to you again, Mayonna," he said.

"I'm willing to continue this relationship, but you have to handle the Renee situation immediately," she said.

"I already did, I told her to never, ever contact me or come in the office again, we are no longer friends." Mayonna listened, then responded and asked him,

"How did she take that?"

"She told me; "You will never be with Mayonna again, you belong to me." He said Rene said.

"Well…Michael, it's over and I would like to continue to move forward with you," Mayonna said. "Me too!" he responded.

"Can I call you back?" he asked her. "Sure," she said. They hung up the phone. Mayonna got up feeling better that they discussed the matter. She began to do a few things around the house.

CHAPTER ELEVEN

Tragedy

She finished what she was doing and decided to call him back. He didn't answer. She called again, and he picked up sounding like he was in extreme pain.

"What's wrong? Are you okay??" she said with concern.

"Uhggggg…Uhgggg"….he groaned.

"I am waiting for the ambulance to come; I was walking in my office and I began to have severe chest pains. I'm on my way….to the doctor. I will call you back once I see what the doctor says." He gasped for air. Mayonna grabbed her chest.

"Oh my God, what hospital are you on your way to, I'm on my way!" she responded.

"I'll be okay, sweetheart. I'll call you once I hear from the doctor, don't worry," he said.

"Please let me know as soon as you speak with the doctor, I'm so worried about you," she said. "I will... Uhggg...." The sounds of pain were louder as he hung up the phone. Mayonna was extremely worried but waited patiently for his call. She continued her daily duties, went to a prep meeting to become aware of Costa Rica's youth. She picked her up something to eat, and thought about Michael the whole time, and prayed he would be alright. She got home, slipped off her shoes, took a shower, and sat on her bed. She looked at her clock and noticed this was the time Michael would normally call her. She walked in the kitchen, got a glass of water, and returned to her bedroom. Her phone rang, and she quickly snatched it thinking it was Michael. She looked at it and saw it was a number she didn't know. She answered.

"Hola."

"Hi Mayonna, this is Renee." Mayonna eyebrows moved inward and her eyes grew big. She was immediately on the defense.

"How did you get my number! And why are you calling me!" she responded with an attitude.

"I got your number out of Michael's phone and I just called to tell you that he is dead!" "What! *Mira, no vuelvas llamarme*! Mayonna yelled at her.

"I don't know what you said, but I just wanted to let you know." Renee said, and she hung up.

Mayonna said to herself;

"Why would she have his phone, what is going on?" Her phone rang again, and it was the music settlements office number. She was confused as to why the music settlement called her.

"Perhaps Michael stopped by his office after he was treated," she thought.

"Hola," she answered.

"Hi Mayonna, it's Kevin, Dr. Taylor's assistant from the music settlement. I've been trying to reach current employees, and former employees, to inform them that Dr. Taylor has passed away this afternoon." he said. Mayonna dropped the phone, fell to her knees. She remembered the last time she saw his *feet*; he was wearing black Nike Air tennis shoes, but she knew he always wore *black dress shoes to his office*. Mayonna heartbeat slowed down. She called Tianna and told her everything that happened. Tianna was there at her home to support her and spent the night with her. Mayonna cried all night long. She received a call the next day of the funeral arrangements date and time, which was Wednesday of that week. Mayonna and Tianna walked in the funeral and saw his body lying in the casket, and Mayonna fell to her knees. Her head was down to the floor, and she started to cry. Her friend Tianna was by her side and rubbed her back. *She couldn't lift her head; she still remembered his black shoes.* She felt something gently grab her face and lift it up and whisper in her ear saying;

"I'm hear. You will always hear my voice." Mayonna imagined hearing Michael's voice, once again sounding like the sound of music, reminding her that he was always with her and that she would be forever special to him. Her friend helped her up off of the floor, she looked to the left and saw Renee looking at her with an evil smirk on her face. Though Mayonna was grieving, she managed to overhear Renee talking to her friend.

"I told him he would never be with her; he will always belong to me." Renee said. Mayonna looked farther left outside the window of the church where the funeral was held and realized the window was opened and people were walking past on their way in the church to view Michael's body. She suddenly saw a black butterfly flying back and forth above the window seal. Mayonna remembered the black butterfly in the corner of his office. Although she knew what the black butterfly sometime symbolized, which is something bad happening. She saw this as something good in a not so fortunate situation.

CHAPTER TWELVE

Life Goes On

Mayonna lived in Costa Rica and raised her two daughters Juliana and Tianna Conchilla, who she named after her best friend Tianna, and her only son Michael Ben Taylor Jr. She found out she was pregnant with Michael Jr. after the death of Michael Benjamin Taylor and raised him along with her daughters by herself. The girls have grown into beautiful young ladies, who were college graduates. Both girls were close to their mother, and often visited the U.S. to see their dad. Michael was a young adolescent. (Tall, dark, handsome, protective, loving, and genuine just like his father.)

He made sure his mother had everything she needed and often checked on his *hermanas*. His mother, Mayonna, enjoyed her line of work and built a good fortune doing so. She made the best decision to leave the U.S. and teach Spanish youth to play jazz music. It was only supposed to be for a few years; however, she didn't know she would be offered a salary she couldn't refuse to travel the world to teach famous musicians how to read jazz music. She was very fortunate to have a great best friend who moved to

Costa Rica to help her raise her daughters while she travelled.

Her friend Tianna is known as *tia,* but affectionately known by her *el ninos* as *ti ti.* Mayonna was pregnant with Michael Jr. during the time she worked. She took a small break to give birth and took him with her when she began to travel again. He always had a tutor with her, and he was always around music. He grew old enough to stay with his *tia f*or the last few years Mayonna traveled, then she decided to stay in Costa Rica to raise him and be closer with her girls through high school and college. Time went by so fast. Michael and his sisters grew into adults. He loved music as a young boy and wanted to be a singer, but ended up studying at ASWAD (Association for the Study of the Worldwide African Diaspora) at the Universidad Pablo de Olavide in Spain and graduated with his Bachelors, Masters, and Phd in music and business. Michael had grown to be a fine young man of twenty-two years. After college he asked his mother for a down payment to start a music school, Mayonna knew Michael Ben Jr. wanted to do the same things his father had done, but he didn't know it. She allowed him to have the money. Once the school was running well, Michael Ben Jr. sold it and made a major profit, enough fortune to return his mother's money and build another school.

CHAPTER THIRTEEN

The Omen

It was a beautiful day in Costa Rica. Mayonna just finished cleaning her home. Tianna knocked.

"*Hola* Mayonna"

"*Hola* Tianna, what's going on today?"

"*Nada, mama y tu?*"

"*Bien*, I'm a little tired today, *pero bien*."

"I was thinking about you and everything you had to deal with in your life, with you raising your kids and look at you, you did good muy *bien*. The girls are college graduates and Mikey, he's a college graduate, very smart just like his father. He has more wealth *que su padre.* Have you ever told him anything about his father yet? The kid's been asking about his father since he was little. The first time I remember is when he noticed his *hermanas pasando tiempo con sus padre.* Remember he wanted to know why their dad didn't talk to him,or take him anywhere. The kid would ask me while you were away, "why mì *padre* never came for me" Tianna said.

"Tianna, he mentioned it to me again last week. He is supposed to come by later. I will talk to him."

Tianna laughed "You tell the kid when he's a grown man. Why did you wait so long Mayonna? What are you scared of? Is it the omen? Do you think he will die unexpectedly like his dad did?"

"Tianna, you know I don't believe in the omen. Mikey is extremely fortunate, he's blessed."

"It doesn't matter if you believe in it or not, it's real and you know it. Yeah, Mikey is fortunate financially, but his choice of young women. They go crazy over him. A crazy girl will put something on him like that crazy Renee did with Michael if he is not careful. "

"Oh my God Tianna, ya basta! Mikey is not cursed. He's very fortunate." Mayonna was a confident woman and always knew what she wanted, but she was a human being and had doubts from time to time. Although her life's environments brought her to this place in time, she was very in tune with her children, especially her son. When she spoke to Tianna, deep down she was slightly concerned that her Mikey would get involved with a woman who would put a spell on him to try and keep him from being with the one he loved, and end up dying like his father. She still believed the opposite for him no matter how pessimistic her friend was about the situation. Tianna thought she was being a realist about the Omen, but what she didn't realize was how real the power of optimism was and how Mayonna based her life off of positivity. Her parents and two younger sisters died in a car accident when she was only 9 years old, she was raped by her uncle at 11, plus she had dealt with domestic violence. All these conditions had familiarized her with desolate circumstances, but she always secured her family even in situations that looked bleak to most.

"I hope he's paying attention to *que està teniendo relaciones sexuales con,*" Tianna says as she laughs. Mayonna shakes her head and laughs with Tianna as she knows her friend will say anything.

"Mayonna, remember when you worked at the music settlement and you told me that Mike Sr. would say he was going to take care of you one way or the other?" Tianna said.

"Yeah, he did. I would think to myself, what the heck is this man talking about." They both laughed because they thought he was weird, but he wasn't.

"He was really into you, mama. you had him saying things he wouldn't normally say." They laughed.

"Every time I see Mikey I wonder; how did he get here if you said Mike Sr. used a condom" Tianna said.

"We were protected," Mayonna responded.

"Obviously not, he's here," Tianna laughed and Mayonna shrugged her shoulders. "It was meant for him to be here."

"Honestly Tianna, I say to myself- what purpose does my son serve; we didn't intend for him to be here," Mayonna said.

"You two didn't, but someone higher than you and Mike Sr. did."

Mayonna agreed, then they laughed. There was a knock on the door. Mayonna, still laughing while walking to the door, she said,

"It must be Mikey."

CHAPTER FOURTEEN
Surprise

She opens the door and a tall brown skinned man stands there looking like Mike Sr.'s twin and another petite young woman in a suit with a briefcase.

"May I help you?" she asked.

"Yes, is this the home of Mayonna Cochilla?" the woman said.

"It is," she replied.

"My name is Michelle Taylor-Evergreen, and this is my uncle, George Taylor. I am Michael Benjamin Taylor's oldest daughter and the Taylor family attorney, and this is his youngest brother. I have a message for you, may we come in?"

Mayonna looked at her before she responded.

"Prove to me you are his brother and you're an attorney."

George pulled out pictures of them when they were little boys in the Dominican Republic standing next to their other brother, mother, and step farther. Mayonna reflects on when Michael Taylor showed her the very same picture, while he was telling her where he grew up. Michelle proved this by showing her attorney license.

"Ms. Cochilla, you were sent a letter a while ago to come to court in the U.S. We have been trying to track you down, but we couldn't find you, so we decided to look you up in this country and we found you. Michelle said.

Mayonna thought; "This man has been dead for years and he still has unexpected things appearing that has to do with him." "Come in" she said. Tianna yells from the living room.

"Who is it, Mayonna?" Mayonna escorted George and Michelle into her living room and introduced them to her friend. George complimented her on how lovely her home was. She interjected.

"Why are you here!" she said.

"We are not here to bring trouble; I have something that belongs to you. My father Michael Taylor left money for you in an account with your name on it. There was paperwork filed by him for these funds to be left to you if something happened to him. No one can access these funds but you. This money belongs to you," the Michelle explains. She hands her a form with the amount where Mayonna can file and access the release of funds.

"As you know, Ms. Cochilla, my dad was a wealthy man and his remaining assets and estate had been distributed to his me and my sister and the rest of his family. There were special funds set aside for you and your daughters," she said. Mayonna looked at the form and saw a large sum of money next to her name. Money never phased her as she had built her own wealth and managed to make sure her children were cared for. Mayonna looked at Michael's daughter.

"Why are you bringing this to me after all of this time? I saw you a few times around the office when you were younger, but didn't know you were his daughter."

"I understand you and my father had a relationship, and it was said he loved you. No one followed through on giving you these funds, so, after I became a lawyer, I was made aware by my uncle of the money my dad had for you. He told me that my father talked to him about you quite often and told him what he saved for you in case you needed anything, and he couldn't get to you, so I was able to. Since I became an attorney, I began representing my family's affairs and finances. My uncle asked me to make sure all legalities were in order and to help him deliver you this message to make sure you received what my father intended for you to have" Michelle explained.

Tianna opened her mouth as usual.

"Damnnnn, Mayonna, how much money are you going to have? We were just laughing at Mike Sr. making that weird comment about taking care of you one way or the other. Damn this is clearly the other! I'm glad I'm your best friend!" Tianna laughed.

"Ms. Cochilla," George said, "my brother would talk to me about you from the first time he grew interest in you, he really, really liked you. He thought he was in love at first sight."

"I told you he was really into you!" Tianna interjected.

"He told me in confidence that if something happened to him, please make sure you got access to this account, so I'm honoring my brothers request." George said. Mayonna looked at him.

"Thank you for coming over seas to deliver me something from someone I loved years ago." she said. The door opened.

CHAPTER FIFTEEN
Michael Benjamin Jr.

Michael Benjamin Jr. walked in the door with a young woman. Tianna looked and said, "Oh shit, the day gets more interesting! *Hola* Mikey"

"*Hola ti, ti, hola madre*, who are these people in here? Michael Jr said. Mayonna never answered his question but stood up and asked him.

"Who is this Mikey?"

"Oh, this is a friend of mine *madre*. I thought I would bring her by to meet you." Michael Jr. responded.

"¡Hola! ¿Còmo te llamas?" said Mayonna.

"Me llama Janet" The young lady responded.

Mucho gusto!.Mayonna grabbed Mikey's hand and walked him over to where he could meet his uncle and sister.

"Mikey, this is your family. This is your father's brother and one of your sisters. When you called earlier today and told me you were coming, I decided to talk to you about your father, and before you walked in, I received a surprise myself. Your father left funds for me, Julianna and Tianna, before he died."

"My dad is dead?" Mikey said.

"Yes, baby, let me finish." "As a kid, I thought he never wanted to come around me." Said Mikey Jr. "No!, Mayonna said, "Let me finish." "

He left this money for us and I knew nothing about it. I never met your father's family, I never got a chance to, but he told me about his mother, father stepfather, and brothers and showed me pictures of them when they were young. He also told me he had two daughters, but I never got a chance to be introduced to them. Your father and I liked each other a lot very quickly, we made love and you were conceived. He had an unexpected heart attack and passed away in the hospital emergency room. I didn't know I was pregnant until a couple of months after he died. I had a job opportunity to come to Costa Rica prior to us getting together. I decided to move here, and I continued my career. After I gave birth to you your *tia* helped me with you and your sisters while I was away. Now, we are here with this three-way surprise. I'm meeting your father's brother and his daughter for the first time like you, and they are delivering funds to us. Michelle is also the Taylor family attorney. Taylor is your father's last name, just like yours. She has a sister; her name is Mya." Mayonna took a deep breath and looked at Mikey. "I know this is a lot to take in at once, but honey say something." she said. Michael Jr. looked at everyone in total confusion. Tianna got up and whispered in Mayonna ear.

"What about the omen?" Tianna said.

"Damn, not now Tianna, one thing at a time. He just walked into a lot and quite frankly the surprise is a lot for me too," Mayonna responded. Mikey looked at Janet and immediately asked her to leave.

"Janet, do you mind leaving me with my family for a while. I will talk to you later"

"Sure, Michael. Call me when you're ready." Janet said. She quietly left the house. Mikey turned to his mother.

"All this time I have wondered and asked about my father as to why he wasn't in my life. I thought he never cared about me, I thought something was wrong with me. Do you know how hard it is for a black man to be without his *padre, madre.*" Mikey yelled.

Mayonna looked at him in surprise as her son had never raised his voice in frustration to her. Her eyes grew bigger, she stared him up and down with a frown on her face.

"Miguel, conozco tu frusterated conmigo, pero bajaras tu tono cuando me hables" Mayonna firmly reprimands him.

"Lo siento madre" said Mikey. He clearly forgot who he was talking to. Disrespect wasn't tolerated in the Cochilla house. George immediately intervened.

"Ms. Cochilla, may I say something to him please."

"Sure" she responded.

"Michael, I'm very happy to meet you, and to know my brother has a son. You are my only nephew, and secondly, from one black man to another, I feel your pain. For a while, your father, me, and our brother went without a father before our mother remarried. Your father was an awesome guy, and from the looks of it your mom is awesome too, and she's done a great job raising you. You're a good man, nothing to be worried about. I don't know anything about you, but it looks like you made some great choices. We have been here long enough. Look, here is my number, call me, man. We can hang out, and you can meet the rest of the family." George said.

By this time, Michelle walked toward Mikey and gave him her number too.

"Call me too, Michael. I can't wait to tell Mya we have a brother and that you look just like daddy." Michelle said. George nodded his head in agreement.

"Thank you. How long are you going to be here?" Mikey asked.

"We're leaving the country in the morning. We came to deliver this information to your mother and planned to go back home." Michelle said.

"I will definitely keep in touch; I want to meet my family." Mikey looked at his mother, "I have a question, mom, was dad Spanish?"

"No. he was a Black man. He and his brothers grew up in the Dominican Republic, so he spoke Spanish well. Why baby?" she replied.

"I just wondered. I would like to know more about him" Mikey said. Michelle and George said good-bye as they walked toward the door, Mayonna followed them and thanked them for honoring their brother and father's request. She also emphasized how nice it was to meet them. They agreed and offered for her and her daughters to visit for the holidays and asked if it were okay if they visited too. She agreed, and they left. She walked back over to her seat, and looked at her bestie for life and said;

"Wow, what an evening. I wasn't expecting this Tianna." Mayonna said.

"You good? you handled this situation like the boss lady that you are"Tianna said.

CHAPTER SIXTEEN

The Omen Revealed

"Come sit next to me son." Mayonna said. Michael walked over to his mother and sat down. She rubbed his back. She asked him questions about Janet, the young lady he came with.

"Mikey tell me about Janet. How did you meet her?" Mayonna said.

"I met her through her sister, she's a friend of mine." Mikey said.

"Are you dating her sister?"

"No, no, *madre* I did date her sister, but not anymore. I think Janet likes me; she gets jealous when I talk to other ladies" Mikey said.

Tianna looked at Mayonna and said;

"Ohhh shit, I told you mama, it's a set up." Mayonna heard Tianna but kept calm in her interest of the young lady. Mikey continued to talk to his mother about Janet.

"*Madre*, one day we stopped for a milkshake after work and she asked me did I believe in friends with benefits? I told her no. She continued to talk to me about how amazing she thought I was and I'm too much of a nice guy, and how dumb her sister was to let me go. Then she started talking about how horny she was and invited me to her house" Mayonna had a straight face, but inside she was thinking "oh shit" like Tianna. Even though she had a doubt, she still believed that her son will not make the decision to sleep with someone because they ask him to

80

like his father did. She believed that the prayers she made since pregnancy were strong enough to have his back. Tianna responded with pessimism as usual, which quickly irritated Mayonna.

"No Miguel, nooo!" Tianna yelled. Mikey looked at his *tia* with a frown on his face.
"What is she talking about *madre*, why is she yelling?" Mayonna continued her conversation with Mikey calmly.

"Did you sleep with her?" Mayonna asked him.

"No *madre*. I'm not sleeping with a woman because she asked me however, there is another woman I've been watching for a while. I finally got the nerve to ask her out and she agreed to go out with me. We have been talking to each other alot. *Madre*, I want you to meet her" mikey said.

"Mikey why did you bring Janet in here to meet me if she was la *amiga*? why are you bringing *her a tu casa de madres*?"

"Madre, she just la *amiga?*"

Tianna looked at Mayonna.

"Just *la amiga,* me and a couple of other *el amigos* were hanging out, and she was there, so came with me. he said, I don't believe that" Tianna said.

"I think she thinks something different. *Miguel*, I'll ask you again. Did you have sex with Janet." Mayonna asked.

"No, I didn't." he said. Mayonna looked at her son in his eyes, and he looked just like his father when he was honest with her about his feelings. Tianna looked at Mayonna and said;

"Mayonna, what are you thinking?"

"I think he's telling me the truth Tia. *Miguel* leave that girl Janet alone. She reminds me of this woman your father had sex with before he was interested in me. She stalked him, and she cursed him to death if he fell in love with any

82

other woman other than her. She was the sister of another woman that he dated for a long time. Your father fell in love with me and she was furious, she was doing everything she could to stop him from being with me. A few days before he died, we argued because the woman was standing across the street from my house screaming your father's name, calling him on his phone, and I felt he was being a jackass, like I thought all men were. He had this look in his eyes when he told me the truth, he did sleep wither, but never intended to lead her on as if it were something more serious.You have that same look. I believe you son." Mayonna said.

"I see, my father had a dark side." Mikey said.

"The dark side was the omen that was put on him and he made the mistake of causing this woman to believe he loved her and it wasn't true, but I refused to believe you would follow the same pattern of leading on a jealous woman." Mayonna said.

"Well *madre* I didn't have sex with her and I'm not. I might with this sis I just told you about. She is sexy AF." Mayonna interjected.

"Okay *Miguel*, I don't need to hear all of that." As soon as she said that to him, she gasped for breath, her mouth was slightly opened, and she clutched her chest. She had an *ah-ha* moment.

"Miguel, Tia, do you know what this means? Mikey was one decision away from continuing the omen. He oversaw his own destiny. His purpose was to break the omen. The decision he made to **not** have sex with Janet broke the omen. Look, she said as she pointed to the window behind Mikey's head. Mikey turned around, and Tianna looked. A *monarch butterfly* was flying around the windowpane.

Made in the USA
Monee, IL
11 January 2021